P9-DTA-938

For Tanja, Monika, and Luka
and in memory of a proud grandfather, Branko Sunajko

First edition for the United States and Canada published in 2005 by
Barron's Educational Series, Inc.

First published in Great Britain in 2005 by Hodder Children's Books, a division
of Hodder Headline Limited, 338 Euston Road, London, NW1 3BH Great Britain

Copyright © 2005 by David Melling

All rights reserved.
No part of this book may be reproduced in any form, by photostat,
microfilm, xerography, or any other means, or incorporated into any
information retrieval system, electronic or mechanical, without
the written permission of the copyright owner.

All inquiries should be addressed to:
Barron's Educational Series, Inc.
250 Wireless Boulevard
Hauppauge, New York 11788
http://www.barronseduc.com

International Standard Book Number 0-7641-5878-3
Library of Congress Catalog Card No. 2004116670

Printed in China
9 8 7 6 5 4 3 2 1

GOOD KNIGHT
SLEEP TIGHT

written and illustrated by

DAVID MELLING

BARRON'S

A NEW SOUND
echoed along the
corridors of the castle.
To the king and queen
was born a
royal princess.

The prince
had a baby sister.

He couldn't see what all the fuss was about.

Among the many
    splendid presents was
        the softest, fluffiest pillow
        in the kingdom.

But one day
    the fat royal cat
    squashed it flat!

The poor princess cried.

And cried.

And cried.

So the king popped over for a little chat with his loyal knight.

"Fill this with something soft and fluffy!" he barked.

"And hurry!"

The knight leapt into action.

He was so quick

there wasn't even enough time

to finish the senter

Deep inside the wild wood prickly bears rubbed their grumbly tummies. "Lunch time!" they slurped.

But it wasn't time for lunch…

Two minutes later the grizzled bears shuffled back into the shadows, rubbing their sore bottoms and mumbling to themselves.

"Well really, it's hardly fair. We just wanted a quick nibble. No need for that ..."

Bear hair lay everywhere!

The knight filled the pillow and gave it to the horse.
"Is this pillow soft enough for the princess?" he asked.
"Neigh!" said the horse. (He thought it was too scratchy.)

Nobody noticed slinky shadows curling around the
tree trunks.

A jumble of wolves howwwled from the trees — they sniffed the knight, they sniffed the horse, they sniffed away.

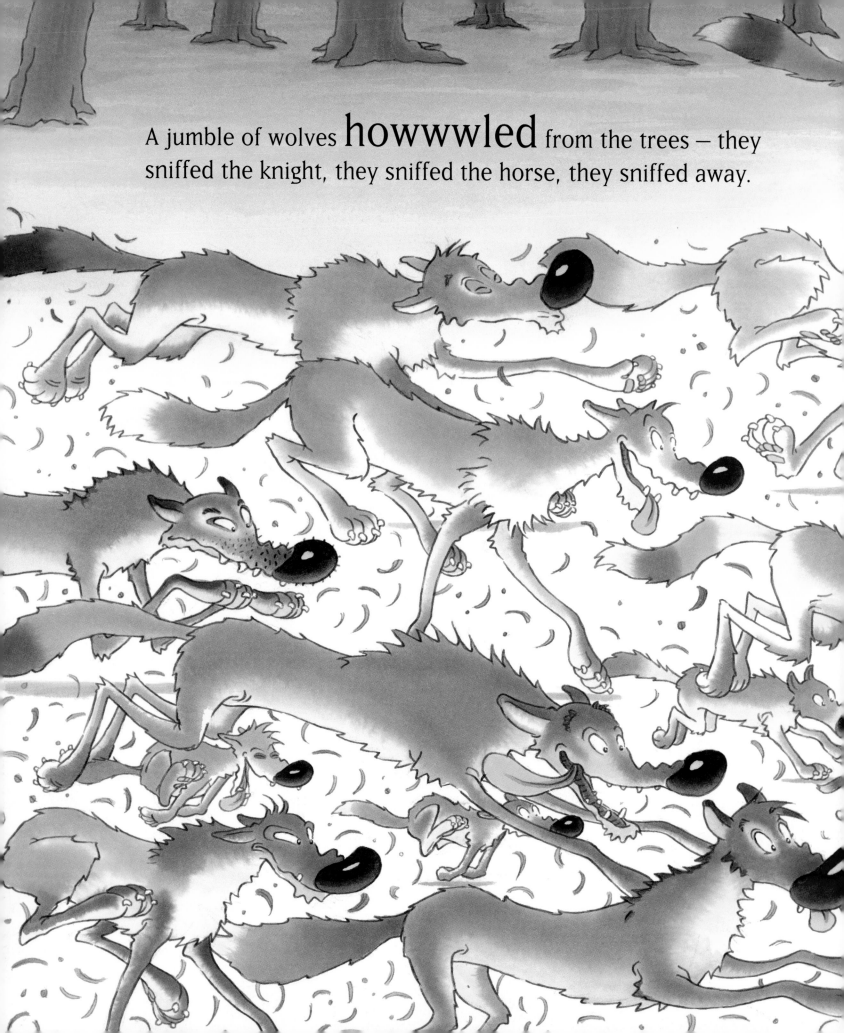

Wolf hair lay everywhere!

The knight filled the pillow again and gave it to the horse.
"Is **this** pillow soft enough for the princess?" he asked.
"Neigh!" said the horse. (He thought it was too bristly.)

Just then...

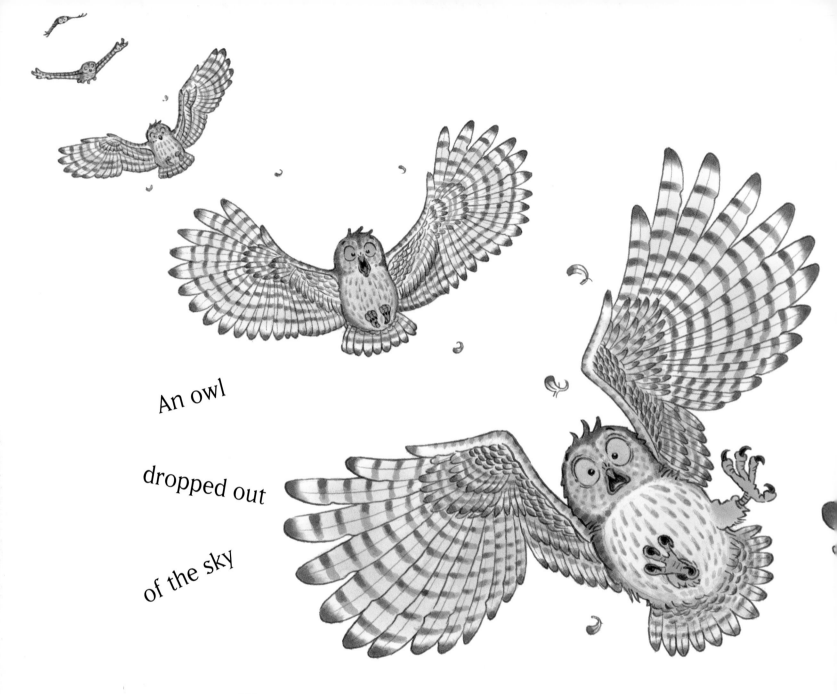

An owl

dropped out

of the sky

and bounced off the knight's head.

Feathers fluttered gently to the floor.

"That's it!" cried the knight.
"I'll make a pillow of feathers!"

"If it's feathers you want,"
said the dizzy owl, "follow me.
I'll take you to see ...

...the Feather Trees!"

So the knight and his **"I'm COMPLETELY scared of heights"** horse clambered up into the branches.

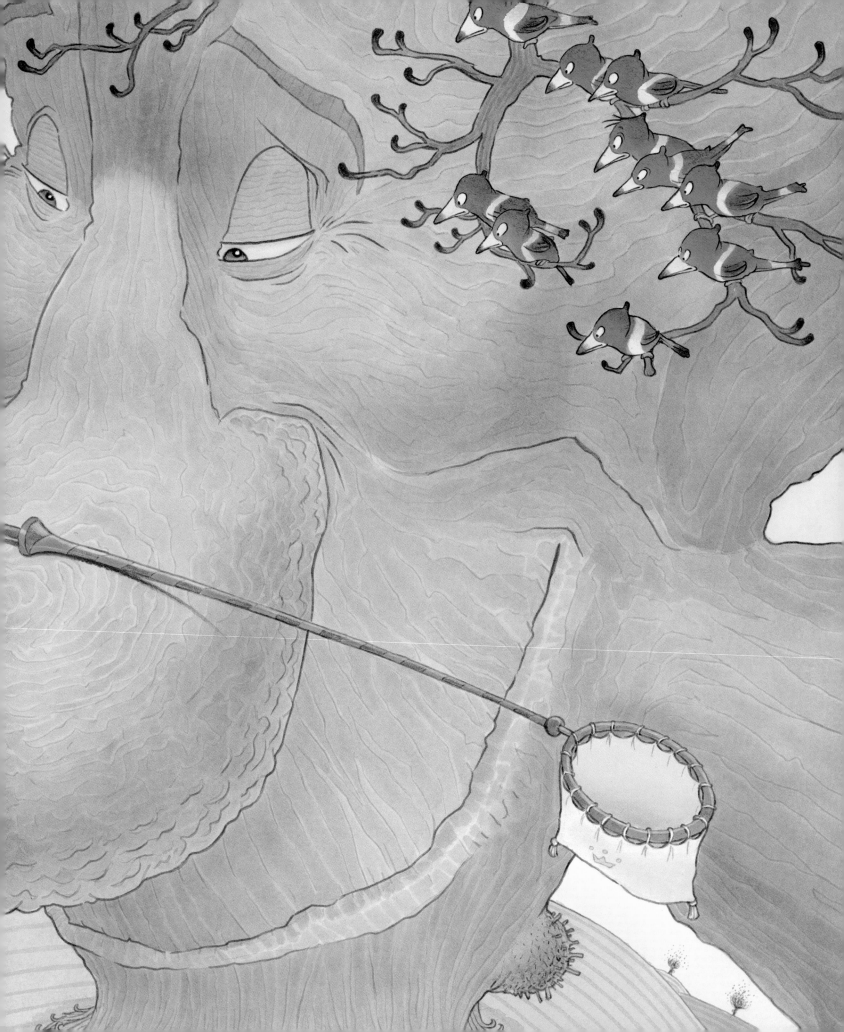

All the birds gathered around to listen
to the knight's tale. There were feathers
everywhere!

When he had finished, the birds happily agreed
to help and plucked just enough feathers to fill
the pillow to the royal brim.

The knight and his faithful horse waved good-bye and galloped and galloped and galloped until they came back to the wild wood.

They wrestled and wriggled their way through its darkest secrets ...

...and plopped out the other side.

No one in the castle had slept for a week, so they
were very pleased to see the knight return.

**"Place that child upon that
pillow before I go bananas!"**

wailed the king.

Everyone held their breath ...

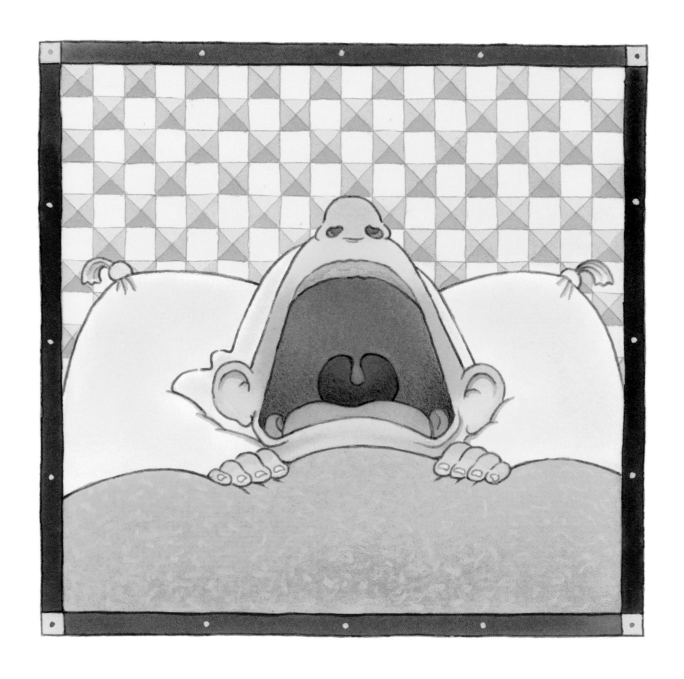

The princess didn't!

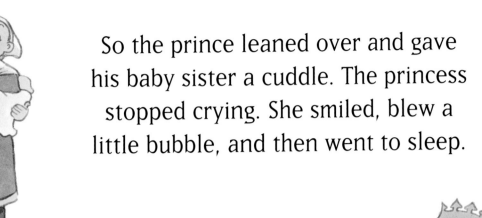

So the prince leaned over and gave his baby sister a cuddle. The princess stopped crying. She smiled, blew a little bubble, and then went to sleep.

The king hugged the prince.

The queen hugged the prince.

At last the castle fell silent ...

…except for the snoring that snuffled,

sleepily through the corridors.

Good knight, sleep tight.